# ARCTIC SPRING

## Sue Vyner

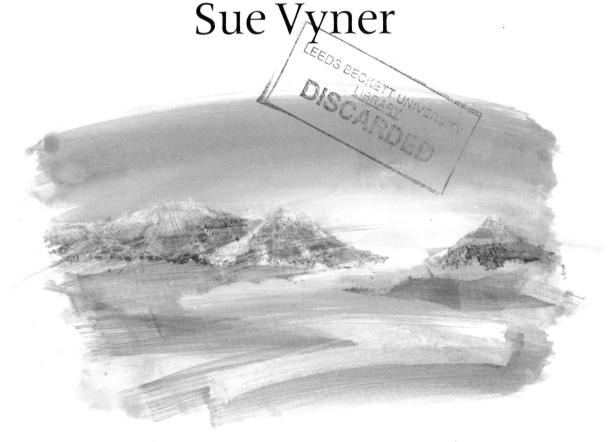

*illustrated by*

# Tim Vyner

GOLLANCZ CHILDREN'S PAPERBACKS · LONDON

The polar bear is snug and warm, asleep in her den in the Arctic snow.

Outside a storm rages. The wind howls and the snow swirls. Suddenly everything shakes and moves.

Later the polar bear wakes up. Now the long winter darkness is ending, so she climbs out of her den.

As she prowls in the snow she sees that the mass of ice is moving, drifting in the sea.

Back on land, something stirs. Long ears poke through the snow, eyes peer out.

The arctic hare wakes up because the winter darkness
has ended. He hops out of his hole.

The arctic fox, whose thick white fur blends into the snow, is awake too.

He is hungry after the long winter.
The hare quickly hides and the fox slinks by.

Sunlight filters through the ice where the ringed seals swim.

A seal finds an air hole in the ice and surfaces into the light.

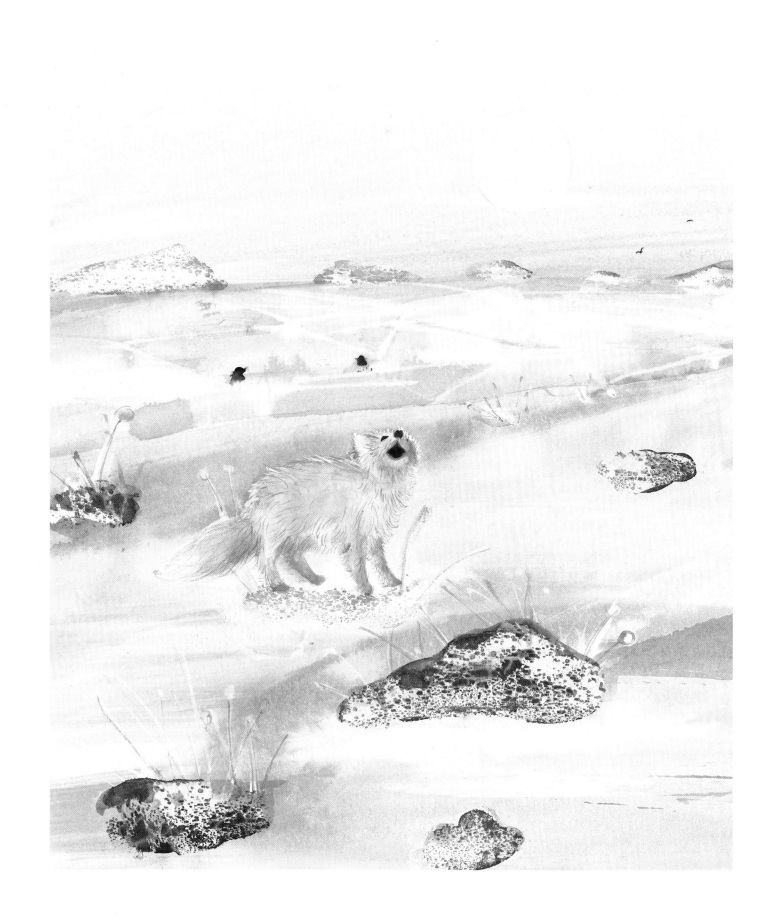

Now the sun shines brightly.

Spring has come to the Arctic.

Out at sea, sunshine bathes the drifting ice
as the birds return.

A long, thin spike sticks out of the sea. A narwhal swims
back to the Arctic to feed.

Strong currents are pulling the drifting ice out to sea.
If it reaches warmer waters it will melt.

The polar bear could swim back to the safety of land,
but she stays on the ice.

A spring wind blows and buffets the polar bear.
Pieces of ice break off and thunder into the sea,

but she stands firm by her den.

When the wind drops, the ice has changed course.
Now it's drifting back towards land.

CRUNCH. With a colossal shudder the ice collides
with the land. Then all is still.

The hare pauses to nibble the poppies which are growing through the snow.

The fox stops, to look for lemmings under the snow.

The seals bask in the sun and the narwhal feeds.

The birds screech and scream as they look for familiar places to build their nests.

Everywhere the snow begins to melt.

In the warmth of the spring sunshine the Arctic flourishes.

The snow shifts around the den. Black, shining eyes blink and stare in the dazzling sun. It is a polar bear cub.

A second cub pushes out of the den and the polar bear
lumbers over to feed them.

Now at last the polar bear can leave her den. In the sunshine of the Arctic spring she sets off with her cubs, to find food and explore the ice and snow.

## POLAR BEAR

The polar bear lives in the Arctic all year round. It has large paws with spiky hairs that help grip the snow and ice, and it is covered with a thick layer of fat for warmth. An excellent swimmer, the polar bear hunts seals. It is the most fearsome animal in the Arctic and the largest meat-eating creature in the world. This bear can weigh as much as half a tonne and can grow to be taller than a man, even when it is on four paws. In winter the male wanders the ice, while the female gives birth to cubs in her den.

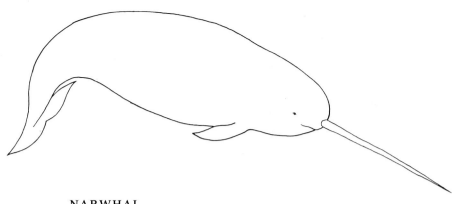

## NARWHAL

The narwhal visits the Arctic in spring and summer. Families or 'pods' feed on small fish at the edge of 'ice floes' — floating sheets of ice. This large mammal weighs slightly less than 2 tonnes and is about 4.5m in length. It is the only whale in the world to have a tusk.

## RINGED SEAL

The Arctic is home to many seals, including the ringed seal. This large mammal is over 1m in length and weighs around 65kg. Clumsy on land, it moves well in water, where it feeds on small fish such as arctic cod. When the seal needs to breathe, it often has to dig through the ice with its teeth and claws to make an air hole. In the spring these seals climb on to the ice and sunbathe for hours.

## ARCTIC FOX

This small fox lives in the Arctic throughout the year. In summer it hunts birds and small mammals such as lemmings, storing away extra food for the winter, when it may even eat grass and berries. Like the arctic hare, this fox's fur turns gray or brown when the snow melts.

## ARCTIC HARE

This hare lives in the Arctic all year round. It is the largest hare in the world, weighing 4.5kg and measuring over half a metre in length. Its paws have special hairs that help it to grip the ice, and in winter it must dig through the snow to find food. The hare's white fur hides it from predators, but when the snow melts, its fur turns gray or brown.

This map shows the Arctic. Most of the Arctic is sea, but around the North Pole, the extreme cold freezes the sea water into great pieces of ice that join together to form pack ice. This floating ice can be up to 6m in depth and can cover an area of over 3000 km wide. Ice also covers the northernmost regions of land within the Arctic Circle.

Large chunks of ice often break off at the edges of these areas and float away until they melt in warmer waters — these are icebergs. Some of the Arctic lands are warm enough for the ice to melt in spring. These lands are the setting for this story.

Text © Sue Vyner 1992    Illustrations © Tim Vyner 1992
First published in Great Britain 1992 by Victor Gollancz Ltd
First Gollancz Children's Paperbacks edition published 1993 by Victor Gollancz
An imprint of Cassell, Villiers House, 41/47 Strand, WC2N 5JE, England
The right of Sue Vyner and Tim Vyner to be identified as authors of this work has been asserted by them in accordance with the Copyright, Designs and Patents Act 1988    A catalogue record for this book is available from the British Library    ISBN 0 575 05528 6    Printed in China by Imago Publishing Ltd